THE TWELVE DOGS OF CHRISTMAS

For Lucy and Siân - AR
To Luquitas, my lovely old buddy - MM

SIMON & SCHUSTER
First published in Great Britain in 2017 by Simon & Schuster UK Ltd
1st Floor, 222 Gray's Inn Road, London, WC1X 8HB • A CBS Company
Text copyright © 2017 Alison Ritchie • Illustrations copyright © 2017
Marisa Morea • The right of Alison Ritchie and Marisa Morea to be
identified as the author and illustrator of this work has been asserted by
them in accordance with the Copyright, Designs and Patents Act, 1988
All rights reserved, including the right of reproduction in whole or in part
in any form • A CIP catalogue record for this book is available from the
British Library upon request • 978-1-47117-823-8 (PB)
978-1-4711-6884-0 (HB) • 978-1-4711-6618-1 (eBook)
Printed in China • 10 9 8 7 6 5 4 3 2

THE TWELVE DOGS OF CHRISTMAS

Alison Ritchie and Marisa Morea

SIMON & SCHUSTER

London   New York   Sydney   Toronto   New Delhi

It's one little pup's first Christmas
and he's ready for some fun.
Everyone seems to be busy –
there are so many things to be done!

Outside he spies two dachshunds
who are trudging to and fro.

It's hard delivering Christmas cards
when you're sinking in the snow!

Something smells deliciously good –
it's next door's Christmas cake.

Three drooling Dalmatians
make sure it's ready to bake!

Now it's time to go and pick the perfect Christmas tree.

Four French bulldogs try to help, but will they all agree?

The bakery in the high street
is filled with scrumptious things.
Five golden retrievers
yearn for five golden rings!

Down at the deli, Christmas treats are piled up on the shelves.

Six Scotties just can't wait . . .
and snaffle a feast for themselves!

Christmas trees in every house sparkle with twinkling light.
Seven stylish spaniels try to make theirs just as bright.

Along the road, a Christmas wreath gives out a festive greeting.

But eight leaping Labradors decide it's there for eating!

DING, DONG, the doorbell rings . . .
it's carol singers outside!

When nine beagles howl along,
the pup just wants to hide!

The Christmas presents are almost wrapped
when somebody comes for tea.
Ten collies help with the gifts
and herd them under the tree!

Out in the park the frosty snowmen
lose their cosy clothes!

Eleven pugs look very well dressed –
and who's found a carrot nose?

Sledges go whizzing down the hill,
zig-zagging in a blur.
Twelve chihuahuas slide and spin
in a tangle of snowy fur.

It's Christmas Eve and everyone's ready to watch the children's play.

But reindeer dogs and elves run riot . . .

and someone jumps on the sleigh!

Peace and quiet descends at last –
this pup has had a ball!

There's one more Christmas treat for him . . . .

. . . the best surprise of all.